Magic
Animal Friends

For Maisie Nolan
in Manchester

Special thanks to Valerie Wilding

ORCHARD BOOKS
338 Euston Road, London NW1 3BH
Orchard Books Australia
Level 17/207 Kent Street, Sydney, NSW 2000
A Paperback Original

First published in 2015 by Orchard Books

A CIP catalogue record for this book is available
from the British Library.

ISBN 978 1 40832 632 9

1 3 5 7 9 8 6 4 2

Printed in Great Britain

The paper and board used in this book are made from wood
from responsible sources.

Orchard Books is a division of Hachette Children's Books,
an Hachette UK company.

www.hachette.co.uk

Rosie Gigglepip's Lucky Escape

Daisy Meadows

ORCHARD

Can you keep a secret? I thought you could!

Then I'll tell you about an enchanted wood.

It lies through the door in the old oak tree,

Let's go there now - just follow me!

We'll find adventure that never ends,

And meet the Magic Animal Friends!

Love
Goldie the Cat

Contents

Contents

CHAPTER ONE

A Visit From Goldie

Lily Hart cradled a guinea pig in her
arms as she waited at the barn door
for her best friend. The tiny animal
peeped happily as Lily gently stroked its
chocolate-brown fur.

"You're almost asleep, Coco!" Lily said,
as the guinea pig's eyes began to close.

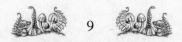

The barn was hidden behind a group of trees in Lily's garden. Mr and Mrs Hart had converted it into the Helping Paw Wildlife Hospital, and all kinds of poorly animals were looked after there. Both Lily and her friend Jess adored animals and loved to help out whenever they could!

Suddenly Lily saw a girl with blonde curly hair and a big grin running towards her. Jess! In moments, Jess was stroking the guinea pig delightedly.

"Coco's leg healed quickly, didn't it?" Jess said happily.

Lily nodded. "But she still seems a bit

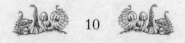

poorly. She's always so sleepy."

They went into the barn, which was filled with hutches of all shapes and sizes. Jess opened the door of an empty hutch, and Lily gently put Coco inside.

The guinea pig squeaked noisily as she crept into a corner and settled in to the

 fresh sawdust.

Lily sighed.

"I'm sure there's something else wrong with her. I wish I knew what. Mum and Dad don't know either."

"And they know everything there is to know about animals," said Jess. Mr and Mrs Hart were both vets. "Maybe she's missing her owner," she suggested.

The girls had spent yesterday putting up notices around Brightley village and knocking on doors to ask if anyone had lost their guinea pig. But no one had. So the girls had named her Coco and Lily's parents agreed that she could live at the hospital until they found her owner.

Lily closed the hutch, then listened. "Did you hear that?" She looked at Jess in excitement. "It sounded like a miaow…"

Jess ran to open the barn door. A beautiful golden cat bounded inside.

"Goldie!" Lily cried.

Goldie was a magical cat and their special friend. She lived in Friendship Forest, a secret world where all the animals could talk!

 13

Lily and Jess bent to stroke her. But Goldie didn't seem as pleased to see them as she usually was. She wasn't purring and her tail was flicking from side to side.

"My kitten Pixie does that when she's upset," said Jess anxiously. "I wonder what Grizelda's done this time?"

Grizelda was a wicked witch who wanted to make all the animals leave Friendship Forest so she could have it for herself. She had four servants to help her – dragons! So far, Lily and Jess had stopped three of the dragons from ruining the forest, but they knew Grizelda still had one more dragon left.

Lily crouched down. "Whatever's happening, we're ready to help," she told the cat. "Take us back to Friendship Forest, Goldie, and then you can tell us what's wrong!"

Goldie mewed up at them. Then she ran out of the barn and across the lawn. Lily and Jess dashed after her, and followed her over the stepping stones that crossed Brightley Stream and led up to the Friendship Tree. Its branches were bare, but as the cat reached it, buds appeared on every twig and burst into leaves as green as Goldie's eyes. A bumblebee buzzed around the yellow flowers that had sprung up under the tree, and birds chased each other through the branches, singing happily.

Goldie pawed at some words carved into the tree's bark. Together, the girls read them aloud: "Friendship Forest!"

A door appeared in the trunk. Jess grasped the leaf-shaped handle and opened it. Golden light shone out, dancing over them like sunbeams.

Goldie stepped through the door. With a thrill, Lily and Jess stooped to follow her.

Their skin tingled like lemonade bubbles as they shrank so they were a little smaller than usual.

But when the golden light faded, the girls gave gasps of horror. Friendship Forest was usually filled with warmth and sunshine, but today it looked completely different. The tree branches thrashed about wildly in a fierce wind and leaves and petals swirled through the air. Rain poured down, splashing in puddles everywhere.

"What's happening?" Lily cried, her dark hair whipping around her face.

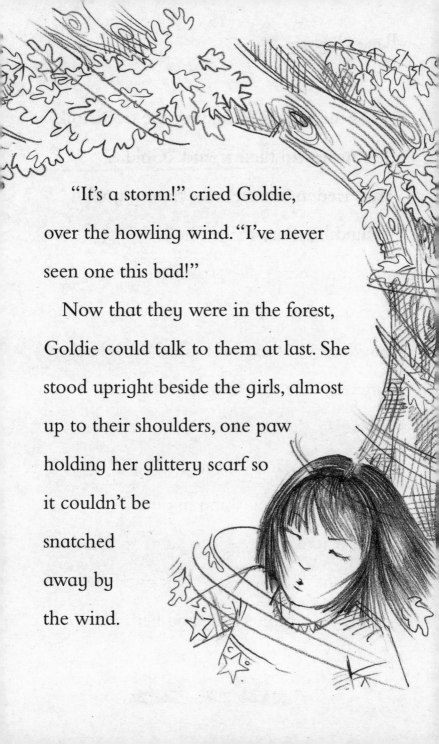

"It's a storm!" cried Goldie, over the howling wind. "I've never seen one this bad!"

Now that they were in the forest, Goldie could talk to them at last. She stood upright beside the girls, almost up to their shoulders, one paw holding her glittery scarf so it couldn't be snatched away by the wind.

As they huddled against the tree trunk, Jess turned to their friend. "Goldie," she cried in alarm, "what's wrong with Friendship Forest?"

CHAPTER TWO

The Terrible Storm

A flash of lightning streaked across the sky. Immediately, a thunderclap boomed around them, making Lily and Jess jump.

"All the animals must be so scared!" cried Lily. "The storm could blow away their houses!"

Goldie nodded, her whiskers quivering

with worry. She reached behind them into a hollow in the tree's roots and pulled out three hooded capes, made of laurel leaves and magnolia petals stitched together.

"I left them here when I went through the tree to fetch you," Goldie shouted over the storm's roar. "They'll protect us from the wind and rain!"

The girls wrapped themselves in the capes thankfully.

"Did Grizelda cause this storm, Goldie?" asked Jess.

"I think so," the cat said. "Remember what she made the other dragons do?"

The girls could hardly forget. Grizelda had made Chilly the ice dragon stop the Flufftail squirrel family from looking after the Shining House, which made the forest sunny. It had quickly become cold and gloomy. Then the Prickleback hedgehog family were turned to stone by Dusty, the sand dragon, so they couldn't keep the river flowing properly with their waterwheel. Next, Smudge the shadow dragon had turned the Fuzzybrush fox family into shadows, so they couldn't dance to make the stars come out.

"Grizelda's still got one dragon left," Jess said with a groan. "Breezy the storm dragon!"

"I think Grizelda's sent her to the Whirligig," said Goldie.

"What's the Whirligig?" asked Lily.

"It's a magical windmill," Goldie explained. "The Gigglepip guinea pig family live there. They turn the sails of the windmill at exactly the right speed to send a lovely, gentle breeze through Friendship Forest."

A gust of wind howled as it swept around them, tugging at their capes.

"That wasn't a gentle breeze!" Lily cried. "Something must have happened to the Gigglepips!"

"Let's go and find out!" yelled Jess.

They hurried through the forest. The little cottages in Toadstool Glade had their doors and windows tightly shut. Conkers were stuffed into chimney tops to stop the rain getting in.

The Longwhiskers rabbit family, who ran the Toadstool Café, were getting soaked as they moved tables, chairs and sunshades indoors. Through the windows, the girls spotted their friends Emily Prickleback the hedgehog and Lola Velvetnose the mole sheltering inside.

A mouse ran across the glade, clutching a tiny umbrella made of ivy leaves.

"Look! There's little Molly Twinkletail!" cried Lily.

Suddenly, the wind caught the umbrella and whisked the tiny mouse into the air.

"Help!" Molly squealed.

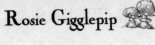

Jess darted

across Toadstool

Glade. She caught

Molly gently.

The little mouse

sat quivering in

her hand. Jess

kissed her tiny

damp head and

lifted her to the

front door of the Twinkletails' cottage,

high up on a tree branch.

"You're safe now, Molly," she said.

"Make sure your family stays inside until

the horrid storm is over."

"Thank you, Jess! I will!" cried Molly,
as her dad opened the door. She ran
inside to a chorus of squeaks and squeals.

"Poor Molly," said Goldie, when
Jess ran back to her and Lily. Her tail
twitched anxiously. "We'd better hurry. If
the storm keeps going, the littlest animals
will be swept away, just like Molly was!"

As the girls struggled through a big
cloud of leaves being swirled around by
the wind, Goldie gasped.

Ahead was a horribly familiar sight.
A yellow-green orb was floating through

the storm towards them!

"Oh no!" cried Jess and Lily together.

With a *cra-ack*, the orb burst in a shower of smelly yellow sparks that hissed as raindrops hit them. In its place stood Grizelda the witch!

CHAPTER THREE

Gigglepips in Trouble

The witch's cloak flapped in the wind, whipping around her purple tunic and tight black trousers. Her green hair waved wildly in the wind, like a nest of snakes.

Grizelda fixed the girls and Goldie with a cold smile. "You interfering girls are too late to stop my plan this time," she

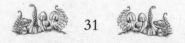

said, looking at them down her long nose. "And so is your silly pet cat."

Jess bravely stepped towards her. "Goldie's not our pet, and she's not silly either!" she cried.

Grizelda just cackled. "I've saved my most powerful dragon for last," she told them. "Ha ha haaa! Thanks to Breezy, this storm will rip every leaf from every tree. All the food growing on the Treasure Tree will be blown to the ground and ruined!"

Jess and Lily looked at each other in dismay. This was dreadful news. The

magical Treasure Tree was where all the
forest animals got their food.

Grizelda pranced in delight. "All the
animals will have to leave," she screeched,
"and the forest will be mine!"

Lily clenched her fists. "We'll stop you,
Grizelda!" she yelled.

"You're too late," Grizelda sneered.

"It's never too late!" Jess shouted over the wind's howl.

"We'll stop the storm somehow," Goldie told the witch. "Lily and Jess are clever and brave, and they won't let you win!"

But Grizelda wasn't even listening. She rubbed her bony hands together. "Kidnapping those dragons was the best thing I ever did!" she crowed. Then she snapped her fingers and disappeared in a

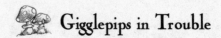

burst of smelly sparks.

The girls and Goldie stood for a

moment, staring at each other miserably.

Goldie said, "Come on. Let's get to the

Whirligig. If there's a way to stop the

storm, I know you two will find it."

The three friends raced through the

forest. They dodged conkers, acorns and

twigs as the wind blew them through the

air, and skidded over the wet leaves that

blew around the ground.

Goldie led them out of the trees to a little hill. On top of it stood a purple and yellow striped windmill with four yellow wooden sails. They were spinning wildly, so fast they were almost a blur.

Goldie gave a gasp. "No wonder the wind is so strong, the sails normally turn

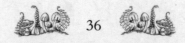

slowly and steadily!" she said. "Only the Gigglepips can work the Whirligig and make the storm stop, but I can't see them anywhere!"

But she had barely finished speaking when faint squeaks reached them through the wind and rain.

"Look!" cried Jess, pointing at a nearby

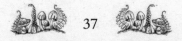

tree. "What is that?"

They peered up into the treetop.

A small column of wind was whirling around on a branch. Through it, they could just see four tiny frightened faces.

"It's a tornado," Goldie cried, "with the

Gigglepip family trapped inside! How can we get them down?"

"Shh," said Lily. She listened hard, straining to hear over the

storm.

"Did you
hear that
squeak? It
sounds closer."

"Help!" a small voice
squeaked sadly. "Help me!"

"Over here!" Lily led them to a low,
thin branch. Clinging to it was a tiny
guinea pig. She looked very wobbly and
frightened. Her wet fur was the colour of
vanilla ice cream, with caramel patches,
and she was wearing a pretty pink rose

on a ribbon around her neck.

Lily gently lifted her down.

"You poor thing," Lily said, cradling the trembling creature in her arms.

"It's Rosie Gigglepip," Goldie said. "It's OK, Rosie. These girls are Jess and Lily, and they've come to help."

Lily wrapped her cape around the shivering guinea pig.

"Thank you," said Rosie, snuggling in.

"Can you tell us what happened?" asked Jess gently.

"It was so scary," Rosie said. "A red dragon flew down and blew at the

Whirligig so hard that the sails started turning too fast. Much too fast! My family tried to slow it down again, but then he blew at us and we went flying up into the air! The wind won't stop until me

and my family slow the Whirligig down again." Rosie's tiny chin wobbled. "I managed to grab that branch," she said, "but my mum and dad, and my sisters, Posie and Josie, were swept up in that swirly wind. I was so frightened!"

Rosie looked at the girls and Goldie with tear-filled brown eyes. "Please help them!" she begged.

CHAPTER FOUR

The Toadstool Café

"We can't climb up to the Gigglepip family," said Goldie. "There aren't any branches low enough."

"Even if we could reach them," said Lily, "I don't know how we'd get them out of that tornado. It's spinning so fast!"

"We must do something," said Jess.

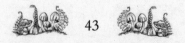

"Let's go to the Toadstool Café and try to think of a plan. Maybe some of the animals sheltering there will know what we can do."

"Good idea!" said Goldie.

Goldie put her paws to her mouth and shouted up to where the Gigglepip family were trapped inside the tornado. "It's alright! Rosie's safe and warm, and we'll find a way to save you soon!"

"Thank you!" A squeaky voice called down through the wind and the rain.

"Don't worry about us," squeaked another Gigglepip, "we're OK, we're just a bit dizzy!"

Lily tucked Rosie inside her cape and they hurried back to Toadstool Glade, dodging swaying branches and the swirls of leaves being tossed around. Just as the Toadstool Café's spotty roof came into sight, there was a roar that bellowed over the sound of the wind.

Lily spun around and gave a cry. "Oh no! Breezy's here!"

The dragon flew overhead, right towards them. She was almost as big as the girls and her red scales glittered in the rain. She playfully swiped some leaves that were being blown about, then opened her mouth.

"Run!" cried Goldie.

They dodged behind a tree trunk just as Breezy blew.

Whoooooooooooooooooooooooooh!

"Hold on!" cried Goldie.

They hid behind the tree as Breezy's powerful blast of wind shot past them. It was so strong that it lifted poor Rosie up into the air. She gave a terrified squeak. Lily reached and caught hold of her paw just in time, but then she felt her own feet being lifted off the ground too!

"We're being blown away!" Lily cried.

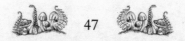

"I'll catch you!" yelled Jess. "Goldie, hold onto me!"

Jess wrapped her arms around the tree trunk and Goldie grabbed on to her. Lily reached out her hand and clutched onto Goldie. Her other hand was still tightly holding onto Rosie's tiny paw. The four friends held each other tight. If they let go, they would be swept away!

At last, the blast of wind died down. Lily's feet touched back onto the ground and she cuddled Rosie.

"Thank you!" squeaked the little guinea pig in a shaky voice.

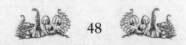

"Thank goodness we are all OK," panted Jess.

But Goldie's eyes were wide with horror. Lily and Jess turned around – and looked at the Toadstool Café in amazement. Breezy's blast of air had blown the café's roof right off!

Lily, Jess and Goldie peered inside the café. Emily Prickleback was staring in shocked surprise as rain sloshed into her honey milkshake. Mrs Longwhiskers tried to protect a tray of cakes from the storm with her apron. Puddles were already

gathering on the wooden floor.

Mr Longwhiskers looked sadly at

his ruined café. "Those dragons are

spoiling everything in our forest," he said. "Whatever can we do?"

Jess groaned as Breezy swooped over Toadstool Glade again. She put her hands on her hips. "Look what you've done, Breezy!" she shouted up at her.

Breezy just giggled and aimed another blast of wind at a tree. All the leaves flew off and swirled around them.

Rosie gave a sob. "I...I...I want my mummy!"

The wind seemed to carry her words up to Breezy. The dragon suddenly looked upset and landed with a thump beside

 51

them. "I miss *my* mummy too," she said miserably.

Lily, Jess and Goldie stared at her in surprise. "Breezy, are you a grown-up dragon?" Lily asked.

Breezy shook her head. "Of course not!" she said. "I'm only little, so my storms aren't big enough for Grizelda. She wants me to make storms as big as my mummy's."

The girls and Goldie looked at each other in amazement. The dragons were only babies!

"There are dragons bigger than

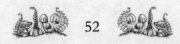

Breezy?" said Rosie, her eyes very wide.

"It sounds like it," said Jess. "Breezy's mum must be huge!"

An idea was starting to come to Lily. "What about Chilly, Dusty and Smudge?" she asked. "Are they babies as well?"

"They're my brothers and my sister," explained Breezy. "We all miss Mummy." She sighed, letting out a puff of air that made the girls' hair blow back and ruffled Goldie's and Rosie's fur.

"Your mummy must miss you too," Jess told Breezy. "Why don't you go home?"

The dragon shook her scaly head. "Can't! Grizelda put a spell on us. We can't fly away from the forest."

Goldie turned to the others, her tail twitching crossly. "Grizelda said she kidnapped the dragons, didn't she? They don't want to be here at all!"

"I know they've caused lots of problems, but I feel sorry for them," said Jess.

Lily nodded. "If we can break Grizelda's spell, I bet they'd go home!"

CHAPTER FIVE

Searching for Spells

When they told Breezy their idea, the dragon shook her scaly head. "No one can stop Grizelda's magic," she said sadly. "We're stuck here forever."

"Well, we're going to try," Jess told her, pushing her windswept curls out of her face. "But first, will you do something for

 55

us? Can you free the Gigglepips from the tornado?"

Rosie's little face peeked out from inside Lily's cape. "Oh, yes!" she squeaked, clasping her paws together. "Please, Breezy!"

But Breezy shook her head sadly. "I only know how to start tornados," she said. "Mummy hasn't shown me how to stop them yet."

Rosie's whiskers drooped with disappointment.

"It's OK," Lily said, cuddling her close. "We'll free them soon, I promise. Now,

where can we find out about dragons and
dragon magic?"

They all thought hard as the wind
swirled around them. Then Rosie gave an
excited squeak.

"I know!" said the little guinea pig.
"Mrs Taptree's library!"

"Brilliant!" cried Jess. "Let's go!"

They hurried through the raging storm,
struggling over broken branches and
weaving through great billowing clouds
of fallen leaves. Only Breezy seemed
to find the journey easy, zipping along
above them. At last, Goldie stopped at

a broad chestnut tree. Its branches were swaying wildly in the storm and it had a door in its trunk. "Here we are!"

Mrs Taptree's chicks, Dig and Tipper, were peering through the window. They waved excitedly and their mother opened the door.

"Come in out of the wind!" Mrs Taptree cried. "Quick! Quick!" Then she caught sight of Breezy, and squawked, "No, no! You'll blow away my books!"

"Breezy will wait outside, Mrs Taptree," said Goldie. She hurriedly explained to the Taptrees why they'd come. "Have you got any books on dragons?"

"Ladders?" said Mrs Taptree, clapping her wings together. "Dragon books, please! Quick!"

The ladders glided along the shelves. Goldie and the girls collected some books and searched through the pages as fast as they could.

Mrs Taptree closed a book. "This tells you how to clean dragons' teeth," she said. "That's no good."

"I've got *How to Dance Like a Dragon*," said Lily.

"Mine's about teaching dragons to swim," Jess said.

Goldie shut her book. "This is about famous dragons and their daring deeds," she said.

But Rosie gave another excited squeak. "Look!" she cried. "I've found a spell to summon dragons!"

Jess glanced outside at the wild storm.

"I think there already too many dragons in Friendship Forest, Rosie. We don't need any more!"

Rosie frowned thoughtfully. "No, wait," she said. "Grizelda's spell stops the dragons flying away from the forest…but maybe we could summon their mother to come and get them!"

Goldie's green eyes gleamed. "That's a brilliant idea! Oh, well done, Rosie!"

"And Breezy said her mum could stop the tornado, didn't she?" added Lily. "So if we can do the spell, we can ask her to free the Gigglepips!"

Rosie gave a delighted squeak and clapped her paws together.

Jess studied the book. "Smoke Signal Summoning Spell," she read. "To summon a dragon, you must send clouds of smoke up into the air. It's important to follow a special pattern: Smoke… smoke smoke… smoke…smoke smoke…" She pulled out the little sketchbook and pencil she

always kept in her pocket, and copied down the pattern.

"There's just one problem," Lily said. "Where can we get smoke in the middle of a storm? It's too wet to make a fire."

The little guinea pig squeaked again. "I know where to get smoke!"

"Where?" everyone cried.

Rosie smiled. "From the dragons, of course!"

CHAPTER SIX

Gathering Dragons

"Good luck!" called Mrs Taptree, as the three friends and Rosie stepped back out into the storm.

"Breezy!" Goldie shouted over the noise of the wind. "Breezy, we're ready to try breaking Grizelda's spell!"

The red dragon gave an excited twirl in

the air as she flew over.

"Yippee!" she cried. "I'm going to see Mummy soon!"

Jess laughed. "That's the plan. Grizelda's magic won't let you fly away the forest, so we're going to summon your mum here to take you home. What do you think?"

Breezy gave a roar of delight, and blew a gust of wind so strong it made a tall beech tree shudder.

"To call your mum, we just need you to breathe your fire so we can have some smoke," Goldie explained.

But Breezy's face fell. "Fire?" she said.

"Smoke?" She shook her scaly head. "I'm no good at breathing fire. My brothers and sister are much better than me, and I don't know where they are."

From inside Lily's cape, Rosie gave a sob. "That means I won't see my mummy either! Or my daddy, or my sisters Posie and Josie…"

"Hang on," Jess said. "We've helped all the other dragons – Chilly and Dusty and Smudge – we know where they are!"

Breezy flew a loop-the-loop. "They can make smoke!" she said excitedly.

Goldie grinned at the girls. "Then let's

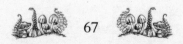

gather some dragons!"

They set off through the storm. Rosie
curled around Lily's neck and peeped out
of the cape hood.

"There!" Goldie shouted over the wind,
pointing to a soft light up ahead. "The
glow-worm bush – that means we've
reached the Winter Cave!"

"Chilly's inside," Lily told Breezy. "Can you call him for us?"

The red dragon flew down, skidding to a stop by the cave entrance. She stuck her nose inside. "Chilly, come with me!" she rumbled. "The girls and Goldie are going to fetch Mummy!"

Chilly came out from the cave, his eyes wide. "Will we really see Mummy again?" he asked.

"We hope so," Jess said.

"Yippee!" shouted Chilly and blew a puff of snow into the air.

"To Coral Cove next!" said Goldie.

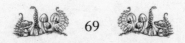

Dusty the yellow dragon loved sunbathing, so Lily and Jess had told her about Coral Cove, a little beach by the river. It was near Grizelda's dark, gloomy tower, so they kept well hidden in the wind-tossed bushes as Breezy told Dusty what was happening.

Then they hurried through the storm to the lighthouse where the Fuzzybrush fox family lived. Smudge the black dragon had loved dancing with Ruby Fuzzybrush, Goldie and the girls so much that little Ruby had asked him to stay with them.

When Smudge came out to join his

brother and sisters, all the Fuzzybrushes
stood at the door, waving.

"Goodbye, Smudge!" Ruby called
over the wind that whistled around the
lighthouse. "Remember the dance moves I
showed you!"

"I will!" Smudge promised. He did a
twirl in the air, but a gust caught his tail
and he bumped into one of the swaying

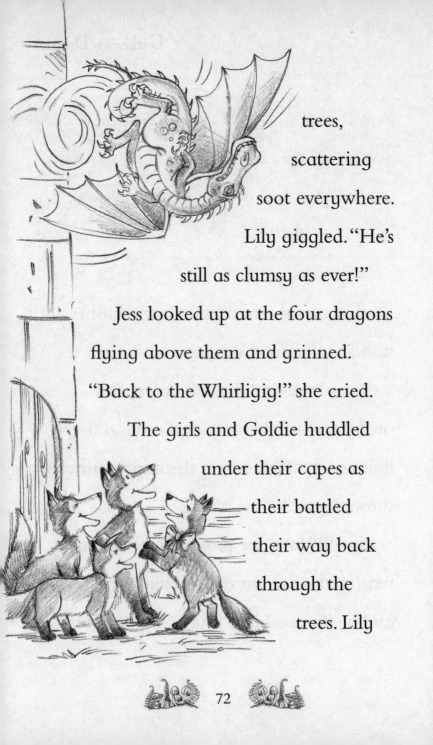

trees,
scattering
soot everywhere.
Lily giggled. "He's
still as clumsy as ever!"
Jess looked up at the four dragons
flying above them and grinned.
"Back to the Whirligig!" she cried.
The girls and Goldie huddled
under their capes as
their battled
their way back
through the
trees. Lily

72

kept Rosie inside her cape, safely tucked under one arm. By the time they reached the magical windmill, the dragons were very excited.

Goldie called up to the Gigglepips, who were still trapped up inside the whirling tornado. "Don't be frightened of the dragons," she shouted, "they're here to help rescue you!"

The four baby dragons landed on the wet ground.

Jess took out her notebook, where she'd written down the smoke-signal pattern. "We need you all to blow big puffs of smoke together," she told Chilly, Dusty and Smudge. "I'll tell you when. And Breezy, we need your wind to blow the smoke straight up. Remember, we don't want any fire, just smoke!"

Dusty looked disappointed. "Not even a little bit of fire?"

Jess shook her head.

"A really tiny bit?" begged Smudge.

"Definitely not," said Lily firmly.

The dragons sighed.

"Everyone ready?" asked Jess. "One… two…three…BLOW!"

CHAPTER SEVEN

Smoke Signals

Chilly, Dusty and Smudge all puffed out their cheeks and blew. Jets of smoke shot out of their mouths, forming a huge dark cloud above them. Then Breezy's wind caught it and the smoke whirled up, higher and higher in the sky.

"BLOW, BLOW!" Jess shouted. The

dragons puffed out two

more clouds of smoke, one following

quickly after the other. After a moment,

Jess yelled, "BLOW!" Then she shouted,

"BLOW! BLOW!" again.

The clouds of smoke rose up high

above the forest.

"Well done,

everyone!" cried Goldie.

The dragons flapped their wings

happily. Breezy did a loop-the-loop and

landed next to her brothers and sister.

Jess grinned. "Now we've just got to

wait for their mum to arrive."

They all stood looking up at the sky.

The wind howled around them, making

Jess and Lily's capes flap. Rosie stood

under the tree where her family were

trapped, her little paws tightly crossed for good luck.

But nothing happened.

Breezy gave a huge sigh that rippled the tops of the trees. "It didn't work," she said sadly. "Mummy isn't coming!"

The four baby dragons huddled together miserably.

"I don't understand," said Lily, shaking her head with dismay. "What did we do wrong?"

"I don't know," said Jess. "But the dragons are still stuck in the forest, and we've got no way of getting the poor

Gigglepip family down…"

Rosie stood by herself, looking wet and forlorn.

Suddenly, Lily's eye was caught by something flying towards them through the rain. She grabbed Jess's arm.

"Look, it did work! She's coming!" Then she gasped. "Oh no – that's not a dragon… It's Grizelda!"

The witch's yellow-green orb floated towards them. As it exploded into stinking yellow sparks, the baby dragons dived under a tree, their wings wrapped around each other.

The sparks cleared, revealing the witch. The wind blew her green hair around her head even more than usual, and her thin, bony face was purple with rage.

"I might have guessed!" Grizelda screeched. "So you pesky girls made those

smoke signals! What were you doing?"

Before anyone could reply, Grizelda spotted the dragons. She pointed at them, sending a jet of hot sparks that made them jump.

"What
are you
doing here?"
she snapped.
"Go and wait in the
dungeon beneath my tower. Now!"

But then a great dark shadow fell over
them all.

Lily and Jess looked up.

A huge dragon was hovering above the
clearing. Her scales were all the colours
of her babies – red, yellow, blue and
black – and she was even bigger than the
Toadstool Café.

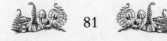

The girls grasped each other's hands.

"Our spell worked after all!" Jess cried. "We've summoned the dragon's mum!"

Lily's eyes were wide. "Jess, do you think we did the right thing? I bet she could burn the whole forest down with one breath if she wanted to!"

"I don't know," said Jess, "but we're about to find out…"

The mother dragon swooped down and landed neatly beside the Whirligig.

"Mummy! Mummy!" yelled the dragons. They flapped over to her, and their mother folded her wings around them.

"My beautiful babies," the mother dragon said in a deep, soft voice. "I'm so happy to see you!"

And she planted a kiss on each of their heads. The baby dragons gave gurgling roars of delight, and snuggled even closer under her wings.

Jess grinned at Lily. "We definitely did the right thing!"

"I've been so worried," the mother dragon said. "Where have you been?"

From the corner of her eye, Lily caught sight of Grizelda tiptoeing away towards the trees.

"I'd forgotten she was there," Lily whispered to her friend.

"Chilly hasn't," Jess giggled. The blue dragon was pointing his wing at Grizelda.

"We were kidnapped," he told his mother. "Kidnapped by her!"

Breezy, Smudge and Dusty flapped over

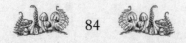

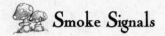

to Grizelda. "Her! It was her!" they cried.

The mother's eyes flashed silver. "Bad!" she thundered. She reared up. With a roar that was far louder than the storm, she blew a stream of red, blue, yellow, black and ice-white flames at the witch.

Grizelda jumped out of the way just in time. She tumbled into a pool of mud and landed with her legs in the air.

"If you come near my babies again," the mother dragon roared, "I'll toast you to a crisp!"

Grizelda scrambled upright. "I'm sorry!" she screeched, staggering as her high heels sank in the mud. Her green hair, covered in brown ooze, stuck to her bony cheeks. "I'm sorry! I'm going!"

With a snap of her fingers, she disappeared in a splatter of smelly sparks.

Everyone cheered. The dragons flew happily around their mother and Lily picked up Rosie and spun her around. The little guinea pig squeaked happily.

"We've defeated Grizelda!" Jess cried.

"Friendship Forest is safe!" Lily chanted.

They grabbed Goldie's paws and danced around each other, not caring about the storm.

The young dragons flapped happily above them, while the mother dragon looked down at the girls.

"I am Saffire," she said. "Thank you for your kindness to my little ones, and for bringing me here. What are your names?"

"I'm Jess, and this is Lily," said Jess. "Our friends are Rosie Gigglepip and Goldie. They live here."

Saffire looked at the trees whipping about in the wind, the snapped branches and fallen leaves. "Breezy!" she bellowed. "Did you make this mess?"

Breezy nodded sheepishly.

Saffire turned to her other babies. "And I suppose you've been spoiling this lovely forest too?"

The young dragons hung their heads.

"Sort of," said Dusty.

"A little bit," said Chilly.

"Well, maybe a lot," admitted Smudge.

"Naughty children!" said Saffire. "If you made the mess, you must clear it up.

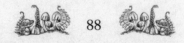

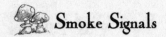

We're not going home until you do."

Rosie
bravely crept
forward and
tapped Saffire's
huge clawed
foot. "Please,

do you think you could help my family?"
She pointed up to the tornado in the tree.
"They've been trapped there for ages,
and Breezy said that you could free them.
Then we can fix the Whirligig and stop
the storm!"

Saffire's great head swooped down until

her big scaly nose almost touched little
Rosie's pink one.

"Of course I'll help, little one," the
mother dragon said.

CHAPTER EIGHT

Surprises

Saffire strode up to the tree where the Gigglepips were trapped. She opened her huge mouth, but instead of a roar, she let out a stream of bubbles. They floated around the tornado, and as they burst in a shimmer of sparkles, the whirling wind vanished. In a flash Mr and Mrs

 91

Gigglepip, Josie and Posie were standing safely on a branch, free at last.

Rosie squealed with delight. "Thank you!" she cried.

Saffire dipped her nose towards the guinea pigs. "Climb on," she said with a smile.

The four Gigglieps hopped onto the dragon's nose, and she carefully lowered them to where Rosie was waiting.

"We're so happy to see you!" cried Mr Gigglepip.

"Thank you so much for looking after Rosie!" said Mrs Gigglepip.

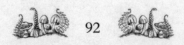

92

"And for saving us!" squeaked Posie
and Josie.

"It's about time we stopped this terrible
storm," said Mr Gigglepip. "Come on –
let's fix the Whirligig. Everyone inside and
hold tight to a whirler!"

Jess and Lily peeped through the
doorway and watched each guinea pig
take hold of a whirler, which was like a
spinning top. Some whirlers were big and

some small, and the Gigglepips darted
from one to the other, spinning them,
stopping them, then spinning again.

"That's complicated!" said Jess. "No
wonder only the Gigglepips can look
after the Whirligig."

The sails began to slow down. As
they did so, the wind began to drop. "It's
working!" cried Lily.

The rain stopped, the sun came out,
and a rainbow arched across the sky. A
soft breeze blew gently through the trees.

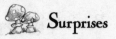

"At last! The storm's over!" said Jess happily, shaking out her tangled curls while Lily shrugged off her cape

"Look," cried Goldie. "All the animals are coming out!"

A family of blue tits flapped their wings dry and turned their faces to the sun. Lola Velvetnose strolled over, whistling cheerfully. Lily and Jess waved as the Prickleback family gathered around the Whirligig, drying off their spines. "Sunshine at last!" called Mrs Prickleback. "Now, what can we do to help clear up?"

Before long, all the forest creatures

were busy tidying the mess made by the storm. The young dragons flew back and forth, taking fallen branches to Mr Cleverfeather, the owl, for him to use in his inventions. Saffire breathed warm air into the Toadstool Café to dry it out, then lifted the roof and put it back on.

As dusk fell, the forest was almost back to normal.

Mr Longwhiskers hopped onto a tree stump. "Everyone's invited to a celebration at the Toadstool Café," he shouted. "And the dragons will be our special guests!"

Soon the girls, Goldie, the Gigglepips,

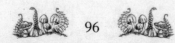

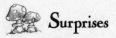

the four baby dragons and all the animals
were sitting around tables outside the
Toadstool Café. Saffire sat nearby,
looking proud and happy.

"My children were very naughty," the
mummy dragon said, "but Jess, Lily and
Goldie understood that Grizelda made
them behave like that. To say thank you, I
have a gift for you all. Look!"

She breathed a long stream of sparks
of every colour imaginable, up into the
darkening sky.

The animals watched, amazed, as the
sparks formed into whirling, spinning,

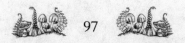

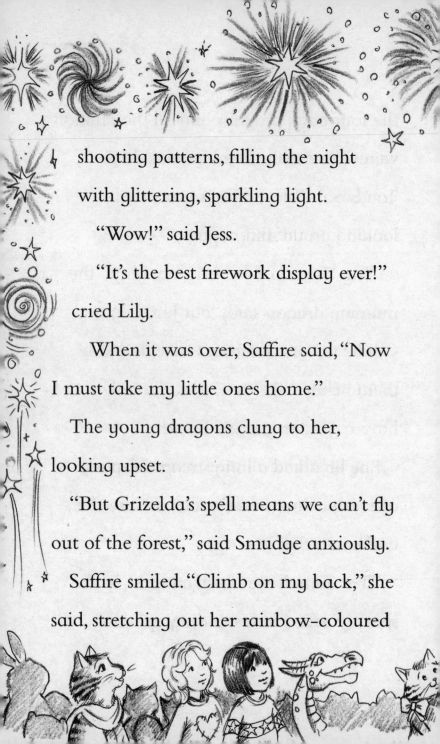

shooting patterns, filling the night
with glittering, sparkling light.

"Wow!" said Jess.

"It's the best firework display ever!"
cried Lily.

When it was over, Saffire said, "Now
I must take my little ones home."

The young dragons clung to her,
looking upset.

"But Grizelda's spell means we can't fly
out of the forest," said Smudge anxiously.

Saffire smiled. "Climb on my back," she
said, stretching out her rainbow-coloured

wings. "No spell can stop *me* flying!"

Moments later, the dragon family soared into the sky, calling, "Bye, Lily and Jess! Bye, Goldie!"

Once they were out of sight, Lily sighed. "I guess it's time for us to go home, too."

She and Jess hugged Rosie, the Gigglepips, and all their other friends. Then, waving goodbye, they followed Goldie through the trees.

"The forest looks lovely again," said Jess. The last raindrops were glittering like diamonds on a starflower bush.

"And look, the Friendship Tree's golden leaves are as beautiful as ever," said Lily, as they arrived.

Goldie took their hands in her paws. "The forest is safe thanks to you!"

Jess and Lily exchanged glances.

"Grizelda will probably come up with a horrible new plan," said Lily.

"But we'll be ready to stop her," added Jess firmly.

Goldie smiled. "I know you will."

She touched a paw to the tree trunk, and a door appeared.

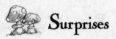

The girls hugged her, then stepped inside, into the shimmering light.

When the golden glow disappeared, Jess and Lily found themselves back in Brightley Meadow.

"What an adventure!" said Jess, as they walked back to Helping Paw.

"It was amazing!" Lily said with a grin. They went into the barn and peeped into Coco's hutch. The guinea pig was asleep in her nest of sweet-smelling hay. But there was something else there, too, nestling beside her.

"She's had a baby!" whispered Lily.

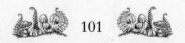

Jess grinned. "So *that's* why she wasn't feeling right!"

The tiny creature was a little smaller than Lily's hand, and had golden-brown fur. She blinked up at the girls.

"She's so pretty!" said Lily.

Just then, Mr and Mrs Hart came into the barn too.

"Mum! Dad!" said Lily. "Guess what? Coco's had a baby!"

Mr and Mrs Hart just smiled.

Lily gasped. "You knew!"

"We wanted it to be a surprise," said Mr Hart, with a grin.

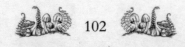 102

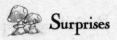

"Jess has her kitten, Pixie," said Mrs Hart, "So we thought it would be nice for you to have a pet, too. Would you like to keep the baby?" she asked. "And Coco, too, of course, if no one claims her."

Lily hugged her parents. "Yes please! Thank you!" she said happily.

Jess was thrilled for her. "What will you call the baby?"

Lily looked at the tiny creature. "Her fur's lovely and golden," she said, "so I think I'll call her Honey – Honey Rose!"

Jess grinned. "Perfect!"

As Mr and Mrs Hart started cleaning

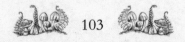

out the other hutches, Coco woke up and nuzzled Honey.

Lily laughed. "She's such a good mum, just like Saffire!"

"I hope Goldie visits us again soon," Jess said.

"Me too," Lily agreed.

They shared a smile. They couldn't wait for their next adventure in Friendship Forest!

The End

It's Goldie's birthday, but wicked witch Grizelda is determined to spoil her party! Can Lily, Jess and little kitten Amelia save the day? Find out in the next adventure,

Amelia Sparklepaw's Party Problem

Turn over for a sneak peek . . .

"Goldie!" Amelia called. "You've got some flowers!"

Goldie came hurrying over. "I've never seen flowers like these before," she said curiously. "I wonder who they could be from. Will you open the envelope, Amelia?"

Amelia tore it open and pulled out a card. The girls and Goldie bent over the little kitten to read it. In scratchy writing, it said:

Dear Goldie,

Wishing you a HORRIBLE birthday!

From Grizelda

Goldie gave a cry of shock.

"That's awful!" cried Lily.

"Trust Grizelda to try to spoil your birthday," said Jess crossly.

As she spoke, the bouquet rustled and the flowers began to grow!

Goldie, Amelia and the girls stepped back, staring in surprise as the beaky flowers grew bigger and bigger...

Read

Amelia Sparklepaw's Party Problem

to find out what happens next!

Puzzle Fun!

Can you help Rosie follow the right path to find her rose ribbon?

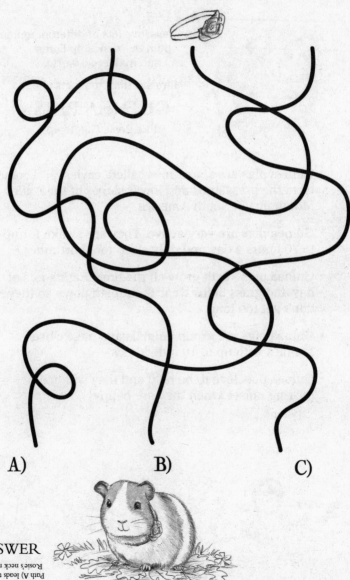

A)   B)   C)

Jess and Lily's Animal Facts

Lily and Jess love lots of different animals –
both in Friendship Forest
and in the real world.

Here are their top facts about

GUINEA PIGS
like Rosie Gigglepip

- Guinea pigs are sometimes called 'cavies' and come
  from the grasslands and lower slopes of the Andes
  Mountains in South America.

- Guinea pigs are very active. They are awake for up
  to 20 hours a day and only sleep for short times.

- Guinea pigs' teeth grow all the time. Eating lots of
  hay and grass helps wear their teeth down so they
  don't get too long.

- Guinea pigs are group animals and have close
  families with up to 10 individuals.

- Guinea pigs love to be held and they will make
  purring noises when they are happy.

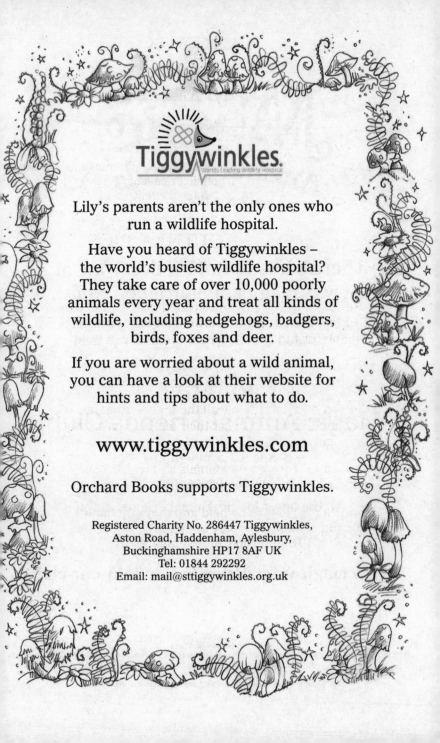

Tiggywinkles.
World's Leading Wildlife Hospital

Lily's parents aren't the only ones who run a wildlife hospital.

Have you heard of Tiggywinkles – the world's busiest wildlife hospital? They take care of over 10,000 poorly animals every year and treat all kinds of wildlife, including hedgehogs, badgers, birds, foxes and deer.

If you are worried about a wild animal, you can have a look at their website for hints and tips about what to do.

www.tiggywinkles.com

Orchard Books supports Tiggywinkles.

Registered Charity No. 286447 Tiggywinkles,
Aston Road, Haddenham, Aylesbury,
Buckinghamshire HP17 8AF UK
Tel: 01844 292292
Email: mail@sttiggywinkles.org.uk

Magic
Animal Friends
Can you keep the secret?

There's lots of fun for everyone at
www.magicanimalfriends.com

Play games and explore the secret world of
Friendship Forest, where animals can talk!

Join the
Magic Animal Friends Club!

-)< Special competitions -)<

-)< Exclusive content -)<

-)< All the latest Magic Animal Friends news! -)<

To join the Club, simply go to

www.magicanimalfriends.com/join-our-club/